christian robinson

an other

Atheneum Books for Young Readers

New York   London   Toronto   Sydney   New Delhi

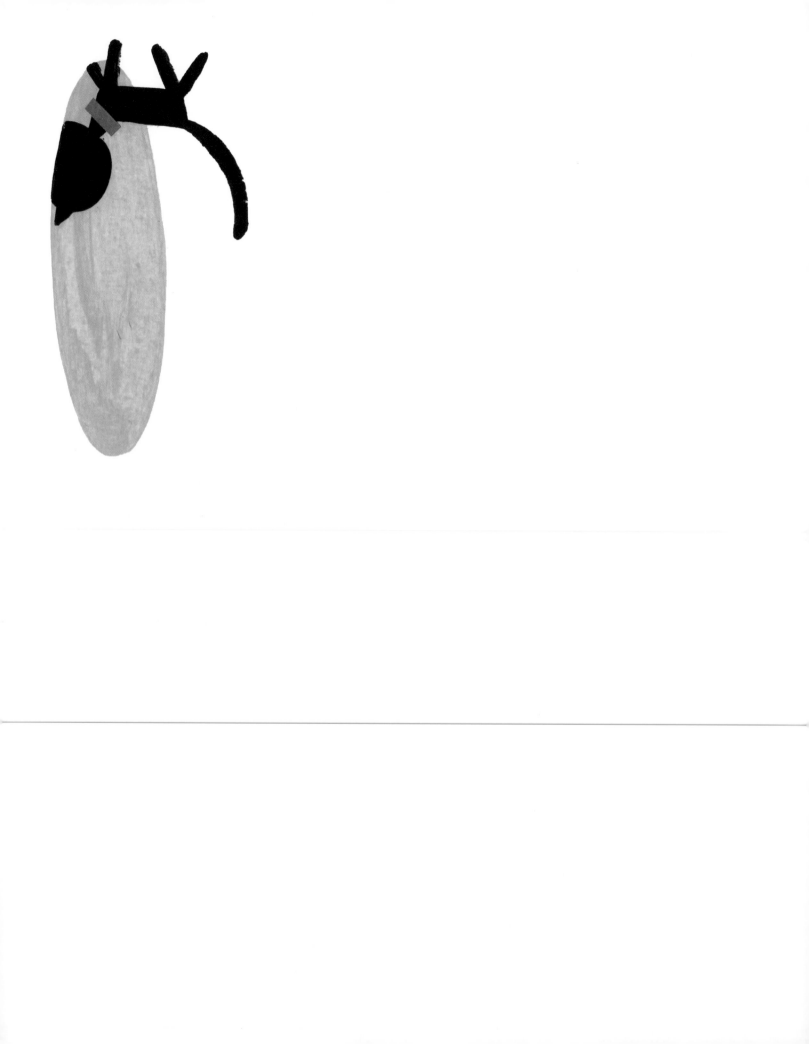

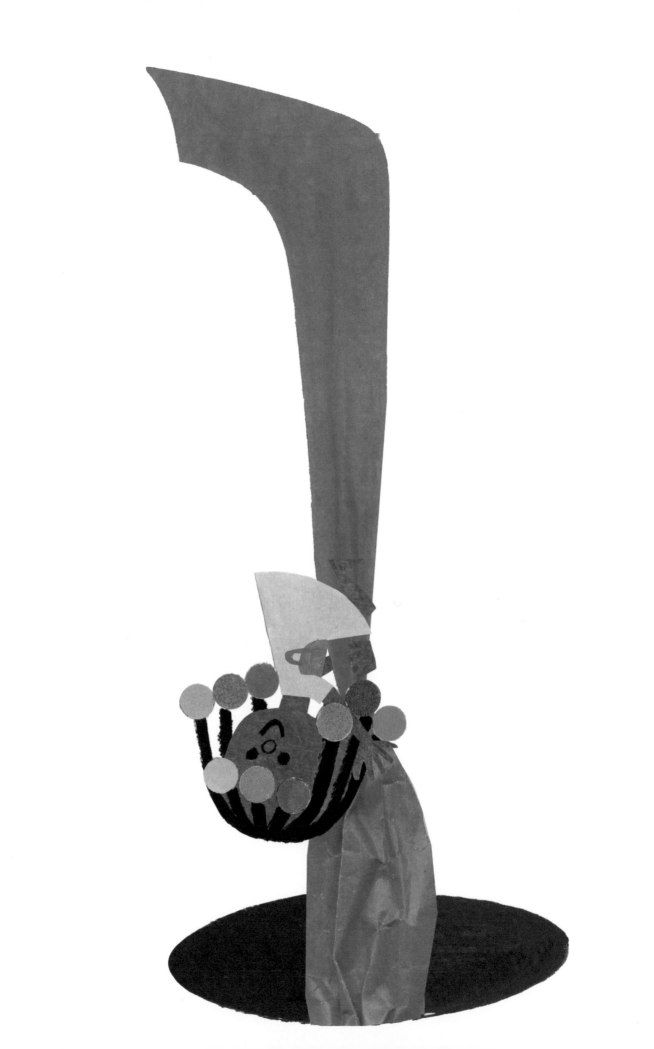

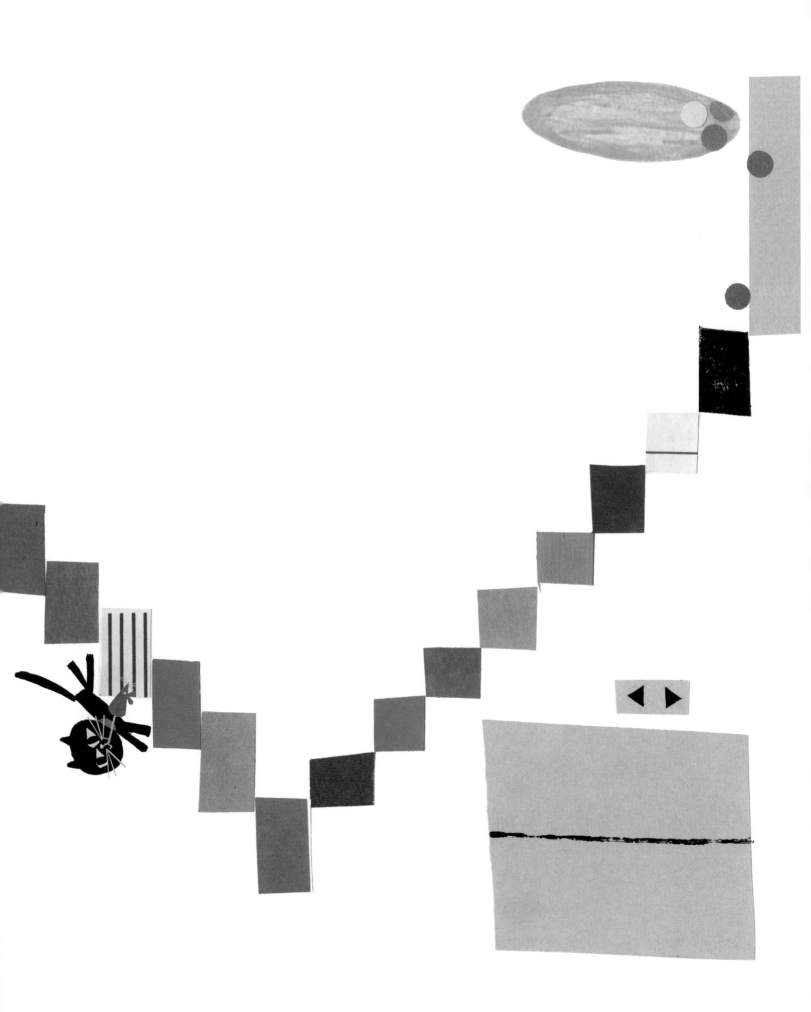

A
atheneum

ATHENEUM BOOKS FOR YOUNG READERS
An imprint of Simon & Schuster Children's Publishing Division
1230 Avenue of the Americas, New York, New York 10020
Copyright © 2019 by Christian Robinson
ATHENEUM BOOKS FOR YOUNG READERS is a registered
trademark of Simon & Schuster, Inc. Atheneum logo is a trademark
of Simon & Schuster, Inc.
For information about special discounts for bulk purchases,
please contact Simon & Schuster Special Sales at 1-866-506-1949
or business@simonandschuster.com.
The Simon & Schuster Speakers Bureau can bring authors to
your live event. For more information or to book an event, contact
the Simon & Schuster Speakers Bureau at 1-866-248-3049 or visit
our website at www.simonspeakers.com.
Book design by Christian Robinson and Ann Bobco
The illustrations for this book were rendered in paint and collage,
with digital editing.
Manufactured in China
1218 SCP
First Edition
10 9 8 7 6 5 4 3 2 1
Library of Congress Cataloging-in-Publication Data
Names: Robinson, Christian, author, illustrator.
Title: Another / Christian Robinson.
Description: First edition. | New York : Atheneum, [2019] |
Summary: "A young girl and her cat take an imaginative journey
into another world"—Provided by publisher.
Identifiers: LCCN 2017057463 | ISBN 9781534421677 (hardcover) |
ISBN 9781534421684 (eBook)
Subjects: | CYAC: Imagination—Fiction. | Voyages and travels—
Fiction. | Cats—Fiction. | Stories without words.
Classification: LCC PZ7.1.R6363 An 2019 | DDC [E]—dc23
LC record available at https://lccn.loc.gov/2017057463

For Steve